W9-BCP-771

Po's Secret Move

adapted by Tina Gallo

Ready-to-Read

Simon Spotlight

New York London Toronto Sydney New Delhi

SIMON SPOTLIGHT
An imprint of Simon & Schuster Children's Publishing Division
1230 Avenue of the Americas, New York, New York 10020

Manufactured in the United States of America 0214 LAK
First Edition
2 4 6 8 10 9 7 5 3 1
ISBN 978-1-4424-9995-9(pbk)
ISBN 978-1-4424-9996-6 (hc)
ISBN 978-1-4424-9997-3 (eBook)

Po was in a great mood.
Today he would start reading
the Sacred Scrolls!
He would finally learn the good stuff
like secret moves and magic defenses.

Po picked up the first scroll.
"How to make . . . tea," he read aloud.
That sounded boring.
"Maybe I can skip ahead
a scroll or two," he said.

“The Sacred Scrolls must be read in the proper order!” Shifu said. “You will take these scrolls to the library and read them all. No skipping, no skimming, no shortcuts!”

Po sat, reading scroll one.
"Besides tea, herbs can be
used to make tiny scented soaps,"
Po read.

"Wow, exciting!" Po said.
Then he sighed.
"Nope. I can't fake it. It's still boring."
He picked up a new scroll.

Po wiggled his fingers as he read. "The Fluttering Finger Mindslip erases the short-term memory of its victim."

Viper came into the room
just as Po was wiggling his fingers.
"Po, I came to tell you—" Viper began.
Then she stopped.
"Hmm. I can't remember.
It must not have been important."

Crane walked into the room next.
"Po, it's your turn to sweep,"
Crane said.
Po wiggled his fingers at him.
Crane blinked.
"What was I saying?" he asked.

Po grinned. "You were saying you
really wanted to sweep,
even though it is my turn.
I will let you do it!"
Crane looked confused,
but he believed Po.
"Thank you. That's
really nice of you."

Tigress entered the room next.
"Po!" she shouted. "Don't be lazy."
Po wiggled his fingers.
"What was I saying?" Tigress asked.

Po grinned. “You asked me if I’d like some tea!”

Next, Monkey asked Po if he
broke his sword.
Po wiggled his fingers at Monkey
and told him he had
broken his own sword.
Monkey believed him.

Mantis yelled at Po for
using his bo staff.
Po wiggled his fingers
and told Mantis he found
his missing bo staff for him.
Mantis believed him!

Po wiggled his fingers
at his friends all day.
"They can't blame me for anything!"
he said to himself.
Po joined the Five at the dining table.

“Who are you?” Tigress shouted.
“What do you mean?” Po asked.
“It’s me, Po!”
Viper smacked Po with her tail.
“Take that, Me-Po!” she said.

"I'm Po! We're friends!" Po shouted.
The Five continued their attack on Po.
Po ran off.
"Do you know who I am?" Monkey asked Tigress.
"No idea," Tigress answered.
Viper screamed. "Where are my legs?"

"I think you are a snake,"
Crane said.
"Oh," Viper said. Then she
screamed again. "I'm a snake!"

Meanwhile, Po told Shifu
what happened.
Shifu was furious.
He hoped there was a way
to bring back everyone's memories.
He and Po would have to look for it.

Po and Shifu went to
the Cave of Mysteries,
searching for a cure.
They found it!
"The Mindslip can be drawn out by
covering heads with clay from the
Pot of Remembrance," Shifu said.

Po asked how to find this Pot.
"By traveling down the Corridor
of Unbelievable Agony,"
Shifu answered.

Shifu gave Po a scroll
with instructions.
Then he left to check on the
Furious Five.
Po was alone.

Po skimmed the instructions.
"I'm going to get that Pot!" he said.
Po raced down the Corridor of
Unbelievable Agony.
Arrows flew at him from every directi-
At the end of the Corridor,
he saw the Pot,
but it was in a cage.

The cage was locked!
"Did I miss something in those directions that I skimmed?"
Po read the scroll again, carefully.
"To unlock the cage, use the key found at the start of the Corridor.
Noooo!" Po screamed.

Po ran back.
He grabbed the key and ran
through the Corridor again.
Finally he had the
Pot of Remembrance.
Po threw the clay on each of his
friends.

Would their memories return?
"You erased my memory!"
Viper said.
"And it's your turn to sweep,"
Crane said.
The Furious Five remembered
everything.

"I'm sorry. I got carried away.
I was being lazy and took shortcuts.
I'm done with that now," Po promised
"How can we be sure?" Mantis asked.
Po would use the memory trick
to erase his own memory.

Po wiggled his fingers
in front of his own face.
“How can we tell if it worked?”
Crane wondered.
Po looked at his friends and blinked.
“Oh wow, the Furious Five!” he shouted.
“Can I have your autographs?
Will you sign my belly?”

"It worked!" the Five said together. Po had forgotten the secret move. They would never have to worry about Po's mind trick again!